KUHLAU

NINE SONATINAS — OPUS 20 & OPUS 55 FOR THE PIANO

EDITED BY WILLARD A. PALMER FROM THE ORIGINAL SOURCES

CONTENTS

Sonatina Opus 20, No. 1 in C Major
    Allegro 2
    Andante 7
    Rondo, Allegro 8

Sonatina Opus 20, No. 2 in G Major
    Allegro 16
    Adagio e sostenuto 22
    Allegro scherzando 26

Sonatina Opus 20, No. 3 in F Major
    Allegro con spirito 32
    Larghetto 38
    Alla Polacca 41

Sonatina Opus 55, No. 1 in C Major
    Allegro 48
    Vivace 50

Sonatina Opus 55, No. 2 in G Major
    Allegretto 54
    Cantabile 56
    Allegro 57

Sonatina Opus 55, No. 3 in C Major
    Allegro con spirito 62
    Allegretto grazioso 65

Sonatina Opus 55, No. 4 in F Major
    Allegro non tanto 70
    Andantino con espressione 73
    Alla Polacca 74

Sonatina Opus 55, No. 5 in D Major
    Tempo di marcia 78
    Vivace assai 81

Sonatina Opus 55, No. 6 in C Major
    Allegro maestoso 85
    Menuetto & Trio 92

Copyright © MCMXCIV by Alfred Publishing Co., Inc.
All rights reserved. Printed in USA.

Cover art: View from The Round Tower of the western part of Copenhagen
by H.G.F. Holm (Danish, 1803–1853?)
Watercolor, ca. 1837
Bodil Bierring Billeder, Copenhagen

    Friedrich Kuhlau was born in Hanover, Germany, on September 11, 1786, and died in Copenhagen, Denmark, on March 12, 1832. His parents moved to Hamburg while he was very young, and there he had the good fortune to study music with Christian Freidrich Gottlob Schwencke, the music director of St. Katherine's church. Schwencke had been a student of the famed Johann Philipp Kirnberger, who studied with Johann Sebastian Bach in the years 1738–41. Thus Kuhlau could boast of a direct musical lineage to the great Bach himself. He also had the distinction of winning the respect and friendship of Beethoven, whom he met during a visit in Vienna in 1825. On that occasion, Beethoven wrote a clever and humorous canon on Kuhlau's name, "*Kuhl, nicht lau,*" (cool, not lukewarm).

    As a young musician, Kuhlau enjoyed a solid reputation as a piano teacher in Hamburg, and gave his first public recital there in 1808. Shortly afterwards, he published his first piano sonatas and several other works. In 1810 Hamburg was annexed to the French Empire, and Kuhlau moved to Copenhagen to avoid conscription into Napoleon's army. His success in Denmark was remarkable. He became a member of the orchestra of the Royal theater, and was allowed to present a concert of his own works. This brought such high acclaim that he was commanded to play before the queen. He wrote a great number of successful operas, and soon became known as "the great Danish composer."

    In 1813 Kuhlau was appointed to a member of the Royal orchestra at the king's court, where he played flute as well as piano. For this he received a rather small salary, but was able to supplement it with his income from his many published compositions. Although he was never married, he retained a large household of relatives, for whose welfare he made himself personally responsible.

    Kuhlau is still widely known for his compositions for flute, and some of his chamber works are still performed. His most valued works are his sonatinas for piano, which are highly valued as study material. These works, composed in the Clementi-Beethoven "legato tradition," are highly expressive, well-constructed works based on classical forms.

Sonatina No. 1
In C Major

F. KUHLAU
Op. 20, No. 1

ⓐ　The slurs in our text are according to the original edition. The breaks between slurs should not be conspicuous.

Rondo
Allegro

ⓐ Here the slurs are editorial. The original edition has none.

ⓐ The forte indication here, missing in other modern editions, is very clearly marked in the original edition.

Sonatina No. 2
In G Major

Op. 20, No. 2

ⓐ The slurs are according to the original edition.

ⓐ *sf* applies to the 1st of the two small notes, which is played *on the beat*. The wedge-shaped staccato marks indicate only that the notes are released instantly. No special emphasis on each note is implied.

ⓑ Played:

17

ⓐ Breaks between slurs should not be conspicuous.
ⓑ This tie, missing in modern editions, is clearly indicated in the original edition.
ⓒ This trill begins on the upper note.

(a) The wedge-shaped staccato marks indicate only that the notes are instantly released. They do not imply any special emphasis.

(b) The small note should be played on the beat, almost simultaneously with the following large note.

ⓐ The trill begins on the upper note.

Sonatina No. 3
In F Major

Op. 20, No. 3

ⓐ The short appoggiaturas are played very quickly, *on the beat*.

Larghetto
sostenuto

(Ped. ad lib..)

ⓐ The small note should be played *on the beat*, and receives the accent.

ⓑ Played:

ⓐ Played, approximately: [etc.]

ⓐ *Polacca* is the Italian word for *Polonaise*. Pieces with the designation *Alla Polacca* are usually brilliant salon works in triple meter, and often they do not retain a great deal of the national Polish style. As is the case with this one, they are frequently bravura technical pieces.

Sonatina No. 1
In C Major

Op. 55, No. 1

ⓐ The slurs and staccato indications in this movement are editorial. The original edition has none.

Sonatina No. 2
In G Major

Op. 55, No. 2

ⓐ Played: [notation] Measure 47 is similarly played.

ⓑ Play the small note very quickly, *on the beat*.

ⓐ Modern editors have changed Kuhlau's text to the following, to agree with the similar passage in measures 13 and 14:

We have retained the original version.

ⓐ Play the small notes very quickly, *on the beat.*

Sonatina No. 3
In C Major

Op. 55, No. 3

ⓐ Play the small notes very quickly, *on the beat*.

Sonatina No. 4
In F Major

Allegro non tanto

Op. 55, No. 4

ⓐ This trill begins on the upper note. Measure 38 is similar.

ⓐ *Polacca* is the Italian word for *Polonaise. Alla Polacca* means *in the style of a polonaise.* This particular composition retains a great deal of the Polish national style; much more than most selections with this title.

ⓑ The small notes are played very quickly, *on the beat,* almost simultaneously with the following large note.

Sonatina No. 5
In D Major

Op. 55, No. 5

ⓐ Most editions have marked this movement legato throughout, which is certainly not according to Kuhlau's intentions. We have retained only the slurs included in the original edition.

ⓑ Play the small notes very quickly, *on the beat.*

Sonatina No. 6
In C Major

Op. 55, No. 6

ⓐ Played: [notation] Measure 82 is similarly played.

ⓐ Played: [musical example] Measure 96 is similarly played.

This page has been purposely left blank.